Gg Hh Ii Jj Kk Ll Mm

Uu Vv Ww Xx Yy Zz

Dear Parent,

The My First Steps to Reading® *series is based on a teaching activity that helps children learn to recognize letters and their sounds. The use of predictable language patterns and repetition of familiar words will also help your child build a basic sight vocabulary. Your child will enjoy watching the characters in the books place imaginative objects in "letter boxes." You and your child can even create and fill your own letter box, using stuffed animals, cut-out pictures, or other objects beginning with the same letter. The things you can do together are limited only by your imagination. Learning letters will be fun—the first important step on the road to reading.*

The Editors

My "e" Book

(This book concentrates on the short "e" sound in the story line.
Words beginning with the long "e" sound are
included at the end of the book.)

written by Jane Belk Moncure

illustrated by Colin King

Little  had a box.

"I will find things that begin with my 'e' sound," he said.

"I will put them into
my sound  box."

Little  found eggs.

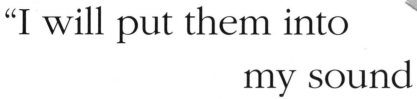

He found lots and lots of eggs.

Did he put the eggs into his box?

He did.

Little  found elves.

The elves danced and danced.

Did Little  put the elves into the box with the eggs?

He did.

The elves played with the eggs.

"Be careful, elves," said Little .

Now the box was heavy.

So Little  found an elephant.

"Hop on," said the elephant.

The elephant went up and down . . .

and the eggs fell out of the box.

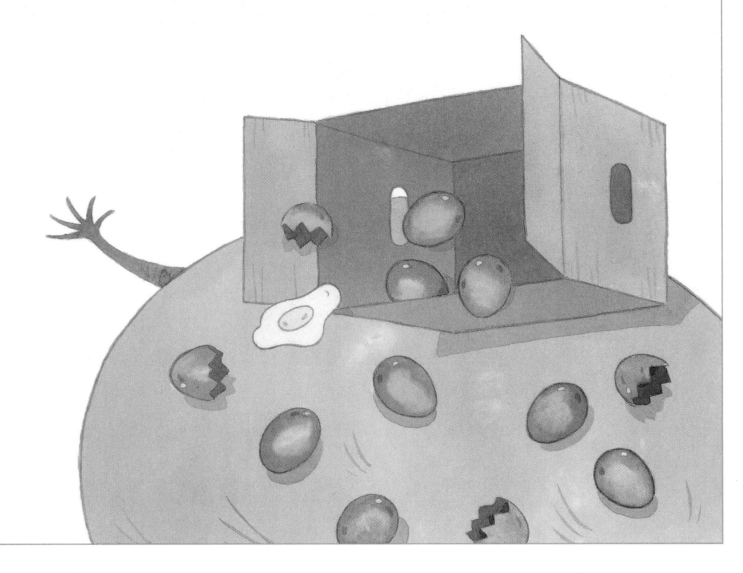

The elves fell, too.

So did Little   .

"That was a bad bump," he said.

"What a mess," said Little .
"Now who will help me
fill my box?"

An Eskimo  came by.

"I will help you
fill your box,"
said the Eskimo.

"I know where we can find lots of eggs," said the Eskimo.

Guess who had eggs,
lots and lots of eggs for Little  ?

Guess who had pretty eggs
for everyone?

elephant

elves

Eskimo

Can you read these words

with Little   ?

elevator

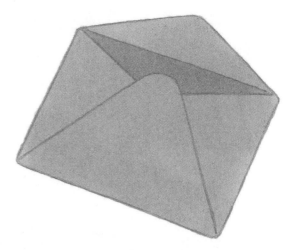

envelope

Little  has another sound in some words. He says his name, "e."

Can you read these words?
Listen for Little e's name.

eagle

eel

emu